Food + Farming

For Rebecca Spens

Copyright © Sarah Garland 1997

Sarah Garland has asserted her right under the
Copyright, Designs and Patents Act, 1988, to be
identified as the author and illustrator of this work

First published in the United Kingdom 1997 by
The Bodley Head Children's Books
Random House, 20 Vauxhall Bridge Road London SW1V 2SA

Random House (Pty) Limited 20 Alfred Street,
Milsons Point, Sydney, New South Wales 2061, Australia

Random House New Zealand Limited,
18 Poland Road, Glenfield, Auckland 10, New Zealand

Random House South Africa (Pty) Limited,
PO Box 337, Bergvlei 2012, South Africa

Random House UK Limited Reg. No. 954009

A CIP catalogue record for this book
is available from the British Library

ISNB 0 370 32373 4

Printed in Hong Kong

Ellie's Breakfast

Sarah Garland

THE BODLEY HEAD
LONDON

Dad !

Come on
Ellie.

It's time for breakfast.

Breakfast for the rabbits.

Breakfast for the turkeys.

Breakfast for the ducks.

Breakfast for the goats.

The goats don't want their breakfast.

The goats want Ellie's hat!

But Ellie needs the hat

to carry the eggs…

to take back home

for Dad to cook...

for Ellie's breakfast.